SPIKE
CHISELTOOTH

Story by
DEIRDRE KESSLER

Pictures by
P. JOHN BURDEN

Ragweed Press
Charlottetown
1989

For Spike

Text © 1989 by Deirdre Kessler
Illustrations © 1989 by P. John Burden
ISBN 0-920304-99-0 (cloth)
ISBN 0-920304-98-2 (paper)
10 9 8 7 6 5 4 3 2 1

With thanks to the Canada Council for its kind support.

Cover Design by Ken Shelton
Book Design by D. Kessler, P.J. Burden and Laurie Brinklow
Typesetting by Braemar Publishing Limited
Printing by Gagné Printing

Ragweed Press
P.O. Box 2023
Charlottetown, Prince Edward Island
Canada C1A 7N7

Distributed by
University of Toronto Press
5201 Dufferin Street
Downsview, Ontario
M3H 5T8

Canadian Cataloguing in Publication Data
Kessler, Deirdre
Spike Chiseltooth
    ISBN 0-920304-99-0 (bound)
    ISBN 0-920304-98-2 (pbk.)
I. Burden, P. John, 1942–   II. Title

PS8571.E87S64 1989 jC813'.54 C89-098550-2
PZ7.K47Sp 1989

In a pet shop, a white baby rabbit huddled by itself. Its sisters and brothers all had been sold. Karl saw the rabbit.

"How much is that little rabbit?" Karl asked.

"It's $9.95," answered the clerk.

"Oh," said Karl. "I have seven dollars. It's my birthday money. That sure is a nice little rabbit."

Karl reached into the rabbit pen and held his hand near the baby rabbit's face. It twitched its nose and nuzzled Karl's hand.

"May I?" asked Karl.

"Sure," answered the clerk.

Karl picked up the little rabbit and held it close.

"Sure is a nice rabbit," said Karl. "And I think it likes me."

"Well," drawled the clerk, studying Karl's face, "since that's the very last one...it's on sale. Seven dollars."

Karl smiled as he left the shop. "I'll call her Spike," he thought, "because her fur is all spikey."

Karl tucked Spike into his jacket and whistled as he made his way home.

He was so absorbed with Spike that he didn't watch where he was going. He bumped smack into Mr. Gribble, the grumpy man who lived in the apartment above him.

"Grumble, grumble," said Mr. Gribble.
"Oh! Excuse me," said Karl.
"Grumble, grumble," said Mr. Gribble.

Karl could see beyond Mr. Gribble's grumbling. "He's just lonely, that's all," he told Spike.

Karl let himself into the apartment where he lived with his parents and two sisters.

"Look, Mom!"

"Where did you get *that*?" asked his mother. "We're not having *that* in the apartment!"

Karl's father looked up from the TV to see what the commotion was.
"You've got half an hour to get rid of it," said his father.

"But, but…," stammered Karl, "…but it's not a cat or a dog! You said I couldn't have a cat or a dog. This is a rabbit. Only a baby rabbit."

"No pets means no pets," said his mother.

"Half an hour," said his father.

Karl went to his bedroom and sat on the bed with Spike. He thought hard. Spike scrambled onto his shoulder to help him think.

Karl had an idea.

With his scout knife he made holes in a box his sister's skates had come in. Then he put his favourite old t-shirt in the bottom of the box.

"My name is Spike," he wrote on the top of the box. "Please look after me because I am an orfan."

Karl crept quietly upstairs to Mr. Gribble's apartment and left the box outside the door.

10

On his way home from shopping Mr. Gribble counted his money carefully.

"Grumble, grumble," said Mr. Gribble. "The checkout person only told me to have a nice day so I wouldn't notice that she'd given me the wrong change."

"Good day, Mr. Gribble," said Mrs. Duggin.

But Mr. Gribble was too busy counting change to greet a neighbour.

"Hello, Mr. Gribble," called Angela, the papergirl.

"Grumble, grumble," said Mr. Gribble. "Two-fifty, two-seventy-five...have a grumble day."

"She was only trying to fool me," he grunted as he climbed the stairs to his apartment.

Mr. Gribble bent over to pick up the newspaper at his door. He noticed the shoebox, picked it up, and let himself into his dreary apartment.

Mr. Gribble set all of the parcels on the kitchen table. Heaving a sigh, he turned to his refrigerator, and an almost pleasant expression crossed his face.

Mr. Gribble loved his refrigerator. It was his best friend. Whenever Mr. Gribble needed comfort, he'd go to his refrigerator and nibble the end of a blood sausage. A mouthful of pickled herring could cheer him on a dark day. His refrigerator never let him down.

Gloating, Mr. Gribble loaded his purchases into the refrigerator.

"Two packages of Limburger cheese, extra strong. Three pounds of blood sausages. One container of head cheese. Five fat slices of liverwurst. One jar of pickled herring with onions in sour cream. That'll do nicely," muttered Mr. Gribble, closing the refrigerator door.

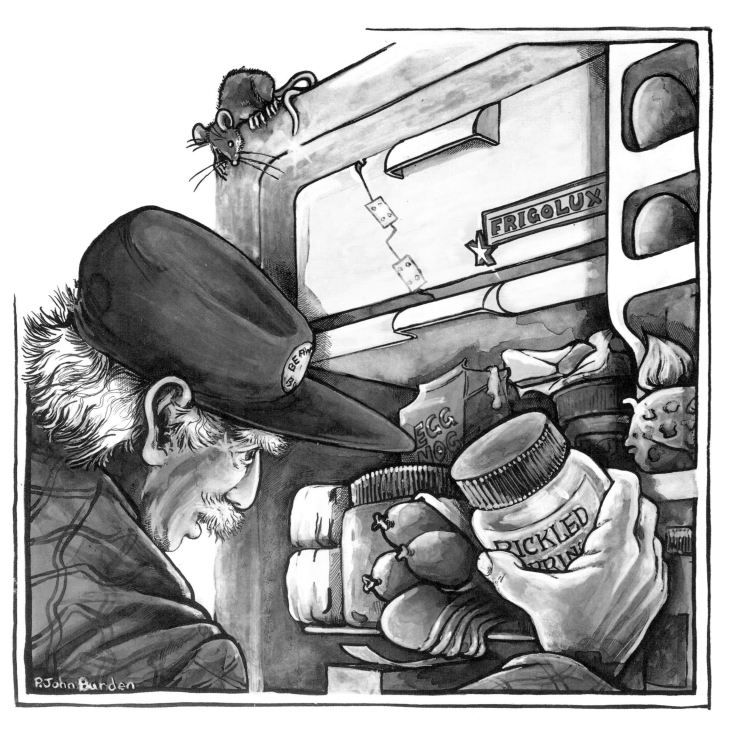

Mr. Gribble turned his attention to the shoebox. He read the note and opened the box.

The little rabbit hunched in the corner. Mr. Gribble lifted it out.

"Grumble, grumble," said Mr. Gribble. "An orphan. The last thing I need is an orphan rabbit."

The baby rabbit pressed close to Mr. Gribble for warmth and pushed its nose into his arm.

"Spike," said Mr. Gribble, setting the rabbit on the floor. "So you are Spike. You'll have to stay the night, I guess. In the morning, though.... Hmmm...where do I take a homeless rabbit?"

Mr. Gribble found a tattered suitcase and put it on the floor in a corner of the kitchen. He propped the lid firmly open and took Karl's t-shirt from the shoebox and arranged it in the suitcase. He put a dish of water beside Spike's new home, then went to the refrigerator to find something for Spike to eat.

"Do rabbits eat pickled herring?" he wondered aloud.

Deciding rabbits probably eat only vegetables and grain, Mr. Gribble poured breakfast cereal in a dish and set it next to the water.

Spike hopped into the suitcase. She wiggled her tail as she snuffed the t-shirt. She found the water and had a little drink. She nibbled a few flakes of cereal.

Spike began to feel at home. She found an empty grocery bag and chewed a big hole in it. She chewed Mr. Gribble's broom. She chewed a corner of a cupboard door. She chewed a pair of rubber gloves, a roll of waxed paper, a wooden brush and a ball of string.

P.John Burden

Spike hopped into Mr. Gribble's bedroom. She chewed a corner of the carpet. She chewed a corner of the closet door. She chewed Mr. Gribble's right slipper and she chewed the elastic on Mr. Gribble's underpants.

"Your name must be Spike Chiseltooth," murmured Mr. Gribble. "Because you do love to chew." A shadow of a smile danced at the corners of his mouth.

As a boy, Mr. Gribble had never been allowed to have a pet. How perfect this little creature was. And from time to time the rabbit would stop, look at him, then hop to his feet and nuzzle his ankles, just as though Mr. Gribble were its mother.

In the apartment below, standing on a chair on top of a trunk piled on his dresser, Karl pressed his ear to a glass which he held to the ceiling.

Spike chewed a bit of everything she could find in the bathroom and the livingroom before she returned to her suitcase and had a nap.

P. John Burden

The very next morning Mr. Gribble went out shopping again. Like a detective, Karl trailed him, unnoticed.

At the pet store, Karl watched Mr. Gribble buy rabbit food pellets and cedar chips for Spike's bedding. At the supermarket Karl watched Mr. Gribble buy carrots and parsley and cauliflower. Mr. Gribble smiled at the girl at the checkout counter.

"It's all for my rabbit," he explained. "I have an orphan rabbit. Just a baby."

Mr. Gribble didn't even look at the change the girl gave him, and when she said, "Have a nice day," Mr. Gribble replied, "Thank you. Have a nice day yourself!"

"Good day, Mrs. Duggin," said Mr. Gribble, passing his neighbour on the street.

"Hello, Angela," he called to the papergirl.

Mr. Gribble was slightly out of breath when he reached the top of the stairs to his apartment. He rushed to open the door, anxious to see Spike.

Spike stopped chewing on the telephone cord and hopped to greet Mr. Gribble. Mr. Gribble picked up Spike and carried her to the kitchen. He sat on the floor with Spike and unpacked the groceries.

"Like carrots, Spike?" asked Mr. Gribble.
Spike nibbled a carrot.

"Like parsley?"
Spike chewed a sprig of parsley.

"This is called cauliflower," said Mr. Gribble, taking a bite of the vegetable himself and holding out a piece for Spike.

Spike chewed the cauliflower. Then she chewed the paper bag. Then she hopped into Mr. Gribble's lap and began to clean herself.

Mr. Gribble sat very still with Spike on his lap. He touched Spike's delicate ears. He felt Spike's sharp claws and strong hind legs. He smiled when Spike's whiskers brushed his arm.

"Welcome to Gribble Towers, Spike," Mr. Gribble said quietly. "I'm glad you've come to stay."

In his haste to see Spike after shopping, Mr. Gribble had left the door to his apartment open. Spike looked up from grooming herself for a moment and then turned towards the door. There was Karl, peeking into the apartment.

"Come in!" called Mr. Gribble.

Karl joined Mr. Gribble and Spike on the floor. Spike hopped into Karl's hands and scrambled to his shoulder.

"She likes you," said Mr. Gribble.

"She likes you, too," said Karl.

"Yes," said Mr. Gribble, "we're her family now. She was an orphan, but now she's a rabbit with a family."

Mr. Gribble held out a carrot to Karl. "Why don't you stay for crunch?" he asked.

Karl and Mr. Gribble looked at each other and smiled.

Spike twitched her nose, waggled her tail, and happily chewed the buttons off Karl's shirt.

The End